ana & andrew

Going to Ghana

by Christine Platt
illustrated by Junissa Bianda

Calico Kid

An Imprint of Magic Wagon
abdobooks.com

About the Author
Christine A. Platt is an author and scholar of African and African-American history. A beloved storyteller of the African diaspora, Christine enjoys writing historical fiction and non-fiction for people of all ages. You can learn more about her and her work at christineaplatt.com.

For the ancestors. —CP

To my number one supporter, Krisna Aditya. —JB

abdobooks.com

Published by Magic Wagon, a division of ABDO, PO Box 398166, Minneapolis, Minnesota 55439. Copyright © 2020 by Abdo Consulting Group, Inc. International copyrights reserved in all countries. No part of this book may be reproduced in any form without written permission from the publisher. Calico Kid™ is a trademark and logo of Magic Wagon.

Printed in the United States of America, North Mankato, Minnesota.
102019
012020

THIS BOOK CONTAINS
RECYCLED MATERIALS

Written by Christine Platt
Illustrated by Junissa Bianda
Edited by Tamara L. Britton
Art Directed by Candice Keimig

Library of Congress Control Number: 2019942033

Publisher's Cataloging-in-Publication Data

Names: Platt, Christine, author. | Bianda, Junissa, illustrator.
Title: Going to Ghana / by Christine Platt ; illustrated by Junissa Bianda.
Description: Minneapolis, Minnesota : Magic Wagon, 2020. | Series: Ana & Andrew
Summary: Ana & Andrew are going to Ghana! Papa is travelling to Ghana and the family gets
    to go too! Ana & Andrew love learning about Ghanaian culture, especially the food!
    While there, they visit Cape Coast Castle to honor their ancestors. There, they learn
    about the origins of the slave trade.
Identifiers: ISBN 9781532136368 (lib. bdg.) | ISBN 9781644942604 (pbk.) | ISBN
    9781532136962 (ebook) | ISBN 9781532137266 (Read-to-Me ebook)
Subjects: LCSH: African American families--Juvenile fiction. | Family vacations--Juvenile
    fiction. | Cape Coast Castle (Cape Coast, Ghana)--Juvenile fiction. | Family history--
    Juvenile fiction. | Slave trade--Africa--History--Juvenile fiction. | Ancestry--Juvenile fiction.
Classification: DDC [E]--dc23

Table of Contents

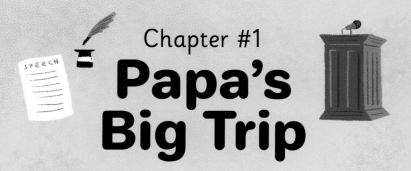

Chapter #1
Papa's Big Trip

Papa had just arrived home from teaching when he said, "I have some exciting news!"

"What is it?" Andrew asked.

"I have been invited to speak at a very special conference." Because he was an educator, Papa often spoke at conferences.

"Sissy and I want to know what makes this conference so special." Ana hugged her favorite dolly.

"*Where* the conference is makes it special." Papa smiled.

"Is it at Disney World?" Ana asked.

"Or in Australia?" Andrew really
wanted to see a kangaroo.

"Let me just tell you," Papa said excitedly. "The conference is in Accra!"

Ana and Andrew looked at other, confused.

"Where's that?" Ana asked.

"Accra is a city, it is the capital of Ghana," Papa explained. "And Ghana is a country on the continent of Africa!"

Papa walked over to their wall map and pointed to Africa. Then, he traced his finger to show them where Ghana and Accra were located.

When Ana and Andrew visited the Smithsonian's Museum of African American History and Culture, they learned about their ancestors from Africa.

"Wow!" Andrew exclaimed.

"Want to know what is even more exciting?" Papa asked. "Guess who's coming with me!"

"Really?" Ana twirled around with Sissy.

Andrew did a wiggle dance. "Woo-hoo! I can't wait!"

"Me either!" Ana hugged Sissy. Then, she pulled Papa and Andrew into her arms. "Group hug!"

Chapter #2
Welcome to Ghana

Ana and Andrew had flown on an airplane to visit their grandparents in Savannah, Georgia. It was a short flight from DC—just a little over an hour.

But traveling to Ghana was very different.

Africa was much farther away. Papa said the flight would take over eleven hours! And because they were traveling outside of the United States, Ana and Andrew needed passports as proof of identification.

ACCRA

"Our first passports!" Ana and Andrew said excitedly as they posed for their photos.

Mama gave them special gifts. Ana's passport holder was covered with illustrations of tiny books. And Andrew's holder had a big red-and-white airplane on the front.

Finally, the big day arrived.

"Guess what?" Ana whispered to Sissy. "We're going to Ghana!"

After checking in at the airport, they waited to board a large plane. Inside was very spacious. The comfy seats even reclined so everyone could relax on the long trip.

Ana and Andrew didn't realize they'd fallen asleep until they heard the pilot say, "Thank you for traveling with us! We hope to see you again soon!"

All throughout the plane, passengers shared their excitement. Many people were speaking languages unfamiliar to Ana and Andrew.

"Are we really here?" Andrew
asked.

"Are we in Africa?" Ana hugged
Sissy tight.

Mama and Papa smiled. "Yes, we
are!"

"Welcome to Ghana!" The pilot
announced.

Papa hailed a taxi to take them to their hotel. When Andrew looked out the taxi's window, he was surprised to see so many buildings and automobiles. Ghana didn't look like the African villages in his picture books.

"Where are all of the wild animals?" Andrew asked.

"And where are the strong women carrying baskets on their heads?" Ana wanted to know.

"Right now, we are still in the city which is very much like DC. But throughout our trip, you will see much more of Ghana," Papa promised.

Chapter #3
Tasty Traditions

The hotel was very fancy. Ana and Andrew couldn't wait to go swimming in the pool. The staff wore uniforms made from colorful printed fabrics. Even the waiters' aprons were colorful unlike the white aprons that servers wore in DC.

One of the waiters carried a large platter to their table. "These are popular Ghanaian foods that you must try! First up is *jollof rice*." She gave everyone a small serving.

Ana and Andrew often ate brown rice. And they'd eaten white rice before. But *jollof rice* was orange.

"Why is the rice that color?" Ana asked.

"Because we add tomato sauce," the waiter explained.

"On the count of three, everyone takes a bite," Mama said. "One, two, three!"

"Delicious!" Everyone agreed.

Andrew did a wiggle dance. "What should we taste next?"

The waiter laughed. "How about *fufu*? See the white puff sitting in the soup? Give it a try."

Ana and Andrew dipped their spoons in the soup and made sure to include a piece of *fufu*.

"Yummy!"

From stews to roasted vegetables, soon everyone's bellies were full of delicious Ghanaian foods.

"Me and Sissy can't eat another bite," Ana said.

"Not even dessert?" The waiter smiled and handed Ana and Andrew a popsicle. "Ghanaian popsicles are stuffed with milk and cookies."

Andrew took a big bite and sighed, "I love Ghana!"

Ana laughed. "Me and Sissy do too!"

Chapter #4
The Castle

The next morning, Papa introduced Ana and Andrew to a man named Kofi Akwasi. "Today, Mr. Akwasi is taking us to visit a castle."

"A castle?" Andrew asked. "Whoa!"

"Yes," Mr. Akwasi said. "A very famous castle. Even former President Barack Obama has visited it."

"Does a king live there?" Ana asked.

Mr. Akwasi smiled. "No. But many African kings once passed through its doors. It is a former slave castle where Africans were held captive before being sold into slavery."

Ana thought about everything she'd learned about slavery. She hugged Sissy. "Where is it?"

"In a nearby city, Cape Coast. But there is no need to be afraid," Mr. Akwasi explained. "Those times have long passed. These days, we visit this castle to honor our ancestors."

Everyone got inside Mr. Akwasi's red minivan and buckled their seat belts. On the drive to Cape Coast, Ana and Andrew looked out the window and counted the colorful fishing boats bobbing in the ocean.

Finally, Mr. Akwasi parked and said, "Here we are. Cape Coast Castle."

Unlike the fairy tale castles that Ana and Andrew read about in storybooks, Cape Coast Castle was made of cold, white stone. And knowing that slaves were once held captive behind its walls was very sad.

"It is important that we be respectful on our tour today," Papa instructed.

"We will," Ana and Andrew whispered.

As they walked through the dimly lit castle, Mama and Papa held Ana and Andrew's hands. Some of the visitors who were touring the slave castle cried and wiped their eyes with tissues.

"There is 'The Door of No Return,'" Mama whispered, pointing at a doorway.

"Why is it called that?" Ana asked.

"Because once enslaved Africans went through that door, they would never return home," Mama said sadly.

"But *you*, their descendants, have returned!" Mr. Akwasi smiled. "And for this, we must celebrate!"

31

That night, Mr. Akwasi hosted a big party in his backyard. His neighbors cooked delicious Ghanaian foods. Everyone wore traditional attire, even Sissy.

As Mr. Akwasi beat a drum and gave thanks, everyone clapped. And throughout the night, Ana and Andrew danced under the stars in honor of their ancestors.